I'm Going To Outer Space!

Written and Illustrated by

Timothy Young

Schiffer Publishing Ltd®

4880 Lower Valley Road • Atglen, PA 19310

This book is dedicated to the incredible visionaries who filled my childhood with amazing visions of the future. To Asimov, Bradbury, Heinlein, Wells, Clarke, Roddenberry, Serling, Lucas, Harryhausen, Spielberg, Adams, and too many more to list.

I'm going to outer space!

I'm just waiting for the
spaceship to come.

I don't know which spaceship is picking me up.

There are so many different kinds!

Once I get to outer space,
the first thing I need to do is get a robot . . .

because everybody in space needs a robot pal.

There are
a lot of things
I want to do in
outer space.

I want to float around in zero gravity.

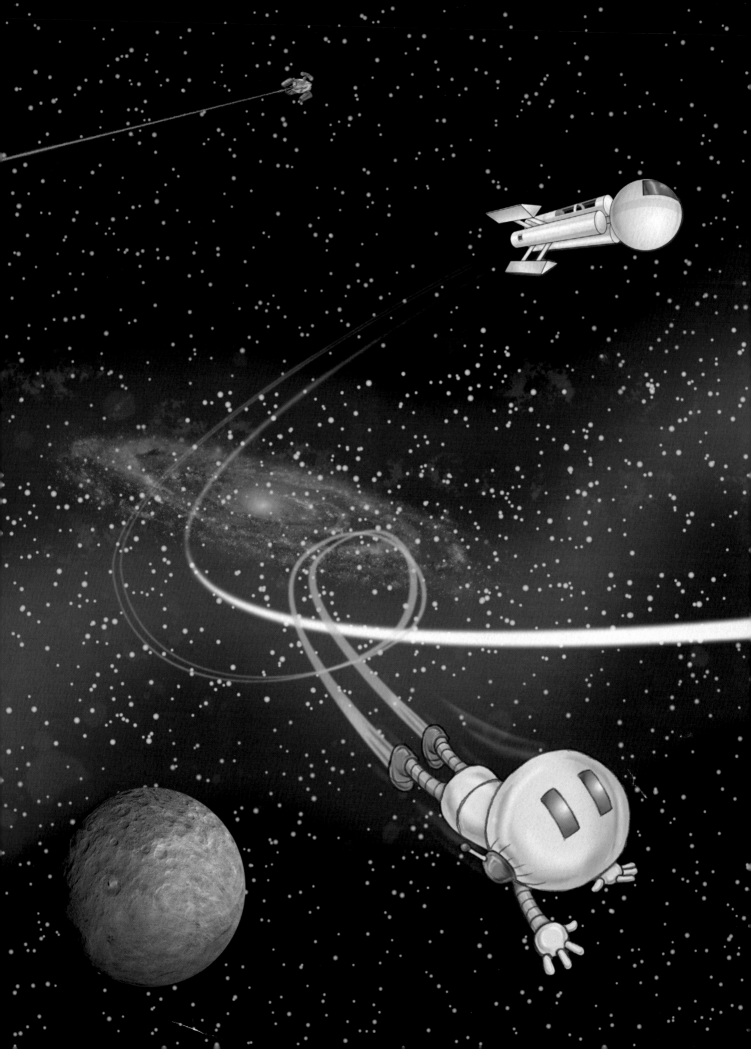

I want to fly through space with a rocket pack!

And I definitely want to visit another planet!

Because I really want to meet a lot of aliens!

I want to meet great big
aliens and really tiny aliens.

I want to meet aliens of all different shapes and sizes and colors . . .

and I'm going to
be friends with
all of them!

I hope my alien friends teach me new games . . . like space-ketball.

I'm going to try as many kinds
of strange and different alien foods as I can.

I'll even eat weird, slimy green stuff!

There's so much to see and do in outer space;
I really hope the spaceship gets here soon.

Oh well, Mom says it's bedtime.

I guess I'll have to wait for a spaceship tomorrow night.

I hope they remember to come.

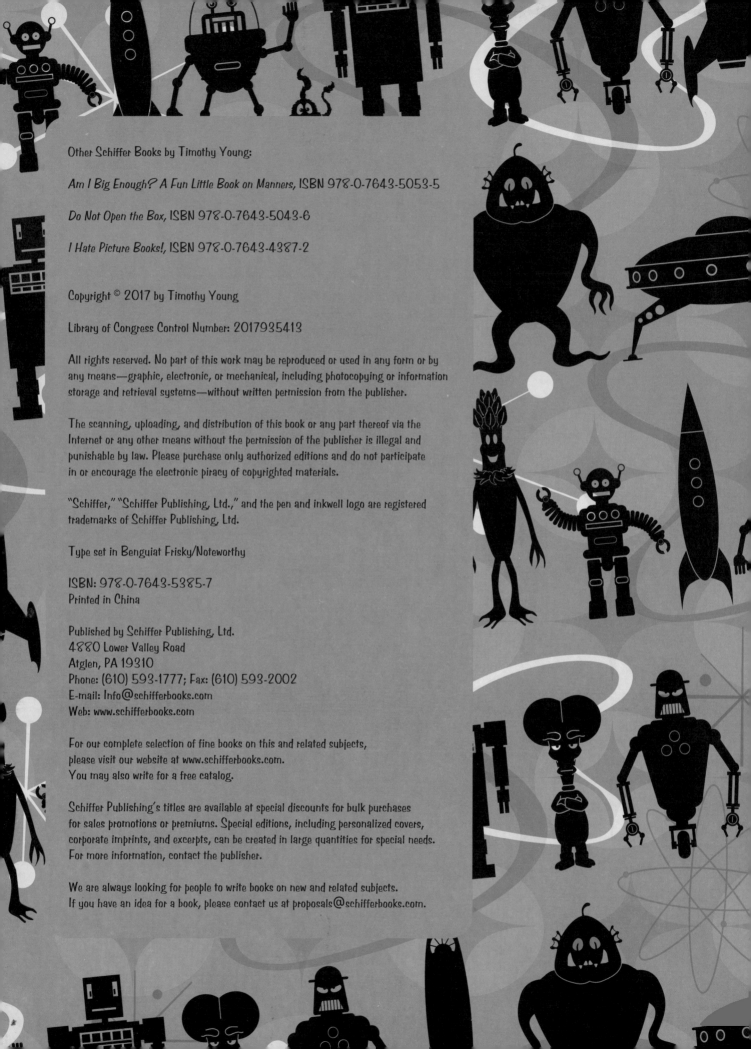

Other Schiffer Books by Timothy Young:

Am I Big Enough? A Fun Little Book on Manners, ISBN 978-0-7643-5053-5

Do Not Open the Box, ISBN 978-0-7643-5043-6

I Hate Picture Books!, ISBN 978-0-7643-4387-2

Type set in Benguiat Frisky/Noteworthy

ISBN: 978-0-7643-5385-7
Printed in China

Published by Schiffer Publishing, Ltd.
4880 Lower Valley Road
Atglen, PA 19310
Phone: (610) 593-1777; Fax: (610) 593-2002
E-mail: Info@schifferbooks.com
Web: www.schifferbooks.com

For our complete selection of fine books on this and related subjects,
please visit our website at www.schifferbooks.com.
You may also write for a free catalog.

Schiffer Publishing's titles are available at special discounts for bulk purchases
for sales promotions or premiums. Special editions, including personalized covers,
corporate imprints, and excerpts, can be created in large quantities for special needs.
For more information, contact the publisher.

We are always looking for people to write books on new and related subjects.
If you have an idea for a book, please contact us at proposals@schifferbooks.com.